The Runaway Bannock

Lou Kuenzler
Illustrated by Greg Gormley

To HP, as there's never any bread in our house – LK

White Wolves series consultant: Sue Ellis,
Centre for Literacy in Primary Education

This book can be used in the White Wolves Guided Reading
programme by readers who need a lot of support in Year 2

First paperback edition 2010
First published 2009 by
A & C Black Publishers Ltd
38 Soho Square, London, W1D 3HB

www.acblack.com

Text copyright © 2009 Lou Kuenzler
Illustrations copyright © 2009 Greg Gormley

The rights of Lou Kouenzler and Greg Gormley to be identified
as the author and illustrator of this work has been asserted by them
in accordance with the Copyrights, Designs and Patents Act 1988.

ISBN 978-1-4081-2213-6

A CIP catalogue for this book is available from the British Library.

This book is produced using paper that is made from wood
grown in managed, sustainable forests. It is natural, renewable
and recyclable. The logging and manufacturing processes conform
to the environmental regulations of the country of origin.

Printed and bound in China by C&C Offset Printing Co.

Chapter One

There once was a little old man and a little old woman. They lived in a little old cottage in Scotland.

The woman was a fine cook.

"I wish I could bake you some bread," she said. "A wee bannock for your tea."

But the little old man and the little old woman were very poor. They had no flour to bake with. Every day, they ate thin cabbage soup.

Then, one evening, a goblin knocked on the door.

"I am very thirsty," he said. "Do you have anything to drink?"

"Only cabbage soup," said the little old man.

"Delicious," said the goblin.

Gulp!

Gulp!

Gulp!

And he drank the whole pot.

Chapter Two

"I love cabbage soup!" smiled the goblin.
He put a big, white sack on the table.
"Here – have this magic flour in return."

"Thank you," said the little old woman. "Now I will bake a wee bannock for our tea."

"Yippee!" cried the little old man.

Soon the bannock was cooked.
"Delicious!" said the little old man.
"I'll eat that bannock in one bite!"

But –

"Oh no, you won't," said the bannock.

Then it jumped up, and ran out of the door.

"Stop!" cried the little old man.

But the bannock kept on running.

It ran down the hill…

And along the lane…

The little old man ran after the bannock. And the little old woman ran after the little old man.

Chapter Three

"Stop!" cried a farmer. "That bannock smells fresh. I'll eat it in one bite!"

"Oh no, you won't," said the bannock.
And it ran through the barn.

The farmer ran after the bannock.

The little old man ran after the farmer.

"That's *my* bannock!" he cried.

And the little old woman ran after the little old man.

A cow and a cockerel and a lady in a big, red bonnet saw the bannock, too.

"Stop!" they cried. "That bannock looks tasty! We'll eat it in one bite."

"Oh no, you won't!" said the bannock.
And it ran past the pond.

The lady rode after the bannock.
The cockerel ran after the lady. The cow
ran after the cockerel. The farmer ran
after the cow. The little old man ran
after the farmer.

"That's *my* bannock!" he cried.

And the little old woman ran after
the little old man.

Chapter Four

The bannock ran around the town...

And over the rooftops...

And through the gardens...
You never saw such a chase!

At last, it got dark. They couldn't chase the bannock any more.

The lady, the cockerel, the cow and the farmer all went home.

The little old man and the little old woman went back to their little old cottage.

26

But the bannock ran on. It ran into a big, dark wood.

"Stop!" said a fox. "The big, dark wood is dangerous. It is not safe for a wee bannock. Rest in my den."

So the bannock stopped.

Gulp!

The fox swallowed it in one bite.

Chapter Five

That *should* be the end of the story.

But, remember, the bannock was baked with *magic* flour.

The flour made the fox's nose tickle.
"A-choo!" sneezed the fox.
And the bannock jumped out of its mouth.

"Stop!" cried the fox.

But the bannock kept on running.

Perhaps it is running still.

Look out of your window.

You might see it now…